SNOTTINGHAM

EXALTED
TOWERS
RESORT

ROCKLAND

HOLO-WOOD
They film movies here.
Everybody seems like
a plastic phoney.

hope to
e who's

OMELETTE

WASTELAND

WATERTON

SWAMP CASTLE

Written by: John Derevlany, Mark Hoffmeier

Creation: AMEET Studio

Scholastic Inc., 557 Broadway,
New York, NY 10012
Scholastic Canada Ltd.,
175 Hilmount Road, Markham
ON L6C 1Z7, Canada
www.scholastic.com

LEGO, the LEGO logo, the Brick and Knob configurations,
the Minifigure and NEXO KNIGHTS are trademarks of the LEGO Group.
©2016 The LEGO Group.

 Produced by AMEET Sp. z o.o.
under license from the LEGO Group.

AMEET Sp. z o.o.
Nowe Sady 6,
94-102 Łódź – Poland
ameet@ameet.pl
www.ameet.pl

Distributed by Scholastic Inc.,
557 Broadway, New York, NY 10012

Please keep the Scholastic Inc. address for future reference.

www.LEGO.com

GREETINGS!

I don't know you, but
you know me . . . I'm

THE BOOK OF MONSTERS!

What will you find in me? Well, for
one thing, I'm full of monsters. Duh.
But I'm also full of magic and notes and
thoughts, and some rotting bits of food.
So, sit back, turn the page, and learn
somethin'! When you've finished, you'll
know almost all you need to know about
the monsters and magic you can use to
become an evil genius. Just remember,
I get all the credit. GOT IT?!

Now, I command you —
GET BUSY READING!

Evilly Yours,

The Book of Monsters

Remind Jestro that
a sandwich is
<u>not a bookmark!</u> — M.

CONTENTS

To all those with honorable intentions who read this — and who frankly can't make head or tails of this contents page — I have left some helpful comments throughout the book so you do not become corrupted by the incorrigibly evil Book of Monsters

— Merlok

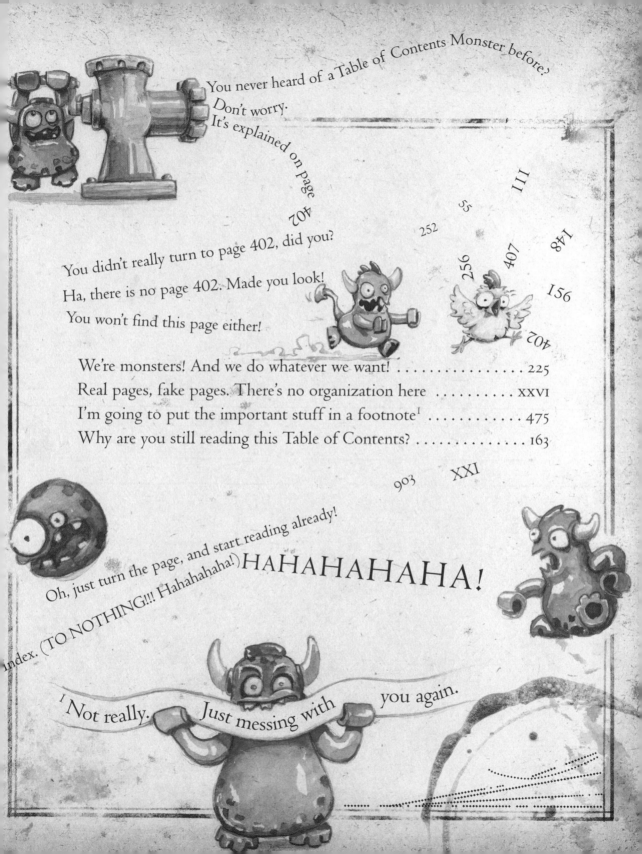

You never heard of a Table of Contents Monster before?

Don't worry.

It's explained on page 402.

You didn't really turn to page 402, did you?

Ha, there is no page 402. Made you look!

You won't find this page either!

55

111

252

256

407

148

156

903   XXI

Oh, just turn the page, and start reading already!

Index. (TO NOTHING!!! Hahahahaha!) HAHAHAHAHA!

[1] Not really.   Just messing with   you again.

Introduction

"So, MR. BOOK OF MONSTERS," you ask. "How did all this get started?" Well, I'm gonna tell you . . .
Time for:

The story of the story behind the story . . .

See, there was this goody-goody wizard, Merlok, always doing happy-happy magic here and nicey-nice magic there. Gag me with a monster.

Blech!

What is this BLECH he speaks of? Did it some kind of evil spell? — M.

Oh, now I get it. BLECH! Like what I said to myself when I read this passage here.

— M.

kay, back to it: What Merlok did long ago was he trapped all the evilness in the realm in a bunch of magic books.

Why? Well, because an evil necromancer had assembled an army and was going to take over the kingdom! Didn't happen.

All thanks to that Mer-loser guy. Merlok made sure this library o' evil was locked up tight.

Me, THE BOOK OF MONSTERS, he kept in a special force field because, well, I AM DANGEROUS! Merlok knows this because he knows who I really am . . .

ne day, Jestro the Royal Jester, tired of being a stinkin' nobody, discovered Merlok's magical books. I convinced the clown to save me. I told him I'd make him good at being bad. We battled Merlok and WON!

Well . . . sort of. Merlok sacrificed himself by creating a huge, magical explosion! It sounded something like this:

Boom!

No, hold on. It was more like . . .

Jestro and I were banished to the other side of the realm, where we started plotting our revenge.

The rest of the magical books had also been scattered to the far corners of the kingdom. Whoever found them would be the big winners in the find-the-magic-books sweepstakes. I had the advantage because I, THE BOOK OF MONSTERS, can sniff out evil books.

Then, it gets even weirder: Merlok became all digital. They named him, Merlok 2.0. He became a sentient computer program! And he recruited a team of doofy, do-gooders called the NEXO Knights — and they fight Jestro and me.

They are not doofy do-gooders. They are

BOOM!

Now, in a world gone mad . . .

Ha! I've always wanted to say that! Any monster banished inside my pages can be unleashed!

The more monsters I make, and the more evil books I devour, the more powerful my evil magic becomes. Pretty soon,

I'll be unstoppable, baby!

One day I, THE BOOK OF MONSTERS, will become so powerful, no army of any kind will stand in my way! It's gonna be . . .

Epic!

Burnzie

Burnzie leads a monster's life. He's a Magma Monster and can be pretty fiery if you cross him — or even if you're just in his way. Burnzie spends most of his time tucked away in me, THE BOOK OF MONSTERS, waiting to be called forth to destroy, destroy, destroy.

It's not totally boring just waiting around in the book. The monsters have Ping-Pong tournaments and set random footnotes on fire sometimes — just for kicks. Burnzie is almost never without his best pal, Sparkks, who also happens to be an extra large Magma Monster.

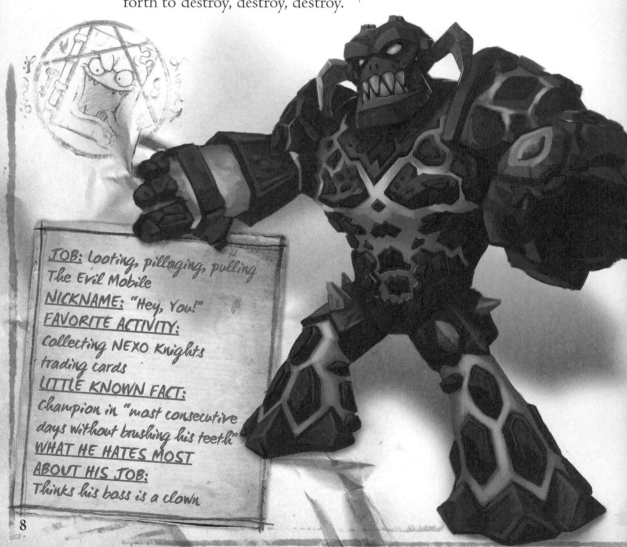

JOB: Looting, pillaging, pulling The Evil Mobile

NICKNAME: "Hey, You!"

FAVORITE ACTIVITY: Collecting NEXO Knights trading cards

LITTLE KNOWN FACT: Champion in "most consecutive days without brushing his teeth"

WHAT HE HATES MOST ABOUT HIS JOB: Thinks his boss is a clown

Sparkks

Sparkks is big — enormous, in fact, and made entirely of magma, 'cause he's a Magma Monster. The one thing he lacks: an ounce of brains. Yup. Except for a couple of pebble-sized bits of magma brains stuck in his brain pan, he's got nothing up there. But, really, does he need a big brain? His daily routine consists of looting and pillaging whatever village is nearby, setting a bunch of stuff on fire, getting distracted by a butterfly, then finally fighting the NEXO Knights — and losing.

JOB: Pillaging, looting, pulling The Evil Mobile

NICKNAME: "Sparkles"

WEAPON OF CHOICE: His fiery breath

LITTLE KNOWN FACT: Hates buying glasses

Burnzie & Sparkks: A Day in the Life

estro loves using these guys! But they're always gettin' destroyed by the NEXO Knights. Every time I cough 'em up out of my pages, they apologize for having screwed up last time. They always promise to do better, but they never do.

I will say, Burnzie and Sparkks have had some pretty crazy adventures together and they always coax Lavaria into drawing pictures of them for their scrapbook.

I LOVE scrapbooking!
Nice work, Monsters!
— M.

Our boss. He loves us. Really...

I even have a Clay Moorington's First Card!

Pillaging, always pillaging...

looting: taking people's stuff.

Pillaging: breaking people's stuff.

Sparkks always loses at Ping-Pong because he has no depth perception.

Burnin' down the hizzouse!
Hip Monsters firin' up the kingdom!

2 MpM (Two Monsters per Mile)

Do we talk about quantum physics while we pull Jestro's wagon? Nope, we mainly talk about rocks. (And sometimes our favorite types of sheep to eat whole.)

Who needs brains? Not us!
We've got Monster-sized muscles!

General Magmar

You want to rule the world with a monster army? You need an amazing general. Magmar's the greatest military strategist and warrior I've ever seen! Fierce. Powerful. And maybe a bit fancy? He uses big words and educated-sounding stuff — like an artist or philosopher.

Most monsters? They growl a lot. Magmar? He enunciates aggressively. I don't even know what he's talking about half the time. Still, he gets the job done a lot better than those other bottom-scratching lava brutes. Plus he's an amazing cook! You have just GOT to try his Magma Chip Cookies.

Magma Chip Cookies Recipe

1. Seize three cups of flour from cupboard.

2. Commence airdrop of magma chips into bowl.

3. Ambush ingredients with mixer until surrender is imminent.

4. Blockade cookie dough cadets in pre-heated oven.

5. Withdraw fully baked vets. Serve with milk.

6. Victory at last!

JOB: Ultimate Monster Warlord
FAVORITE SAYING: "Victory!"
LEAST FAVORITE SAYING:
"Whoops! Lost again!"
WEAPON OF CHOICE:
His very own personal Siege Tower
LITTLE KNOWN FACT:
Loves to cook
GREATEST REGRET:
Always hears his "least favorite saying"

General Magmar
does make a great
Magma Chip Cookie.
Unfortunately,
he's better at making
trouble . . . which is
what he often does.
— M.

Seven Ways to Inspire a Monster Army

1. FLY YOUR MONSTER FLAG PROUDLY

General Magmar raises his flag every morning before the monsters awake. Actually, it's not a flag – it's his old underwear. And it smells TERRIBLE! But monsters love a good stink.

2. ALWAYS SERVE A HEALTHY BREAKFAST

Like . . . scalding lava lumps, oozing slime broth – and taste bud flaying. Oh, yes, and cupcakes.

3. STRATEGY IS EVERYTHING

Magmar's battle maps are brilliant. Troop movements are indicated with bright green arrows. Wait – those aren't arrows! That's where Burnzie blew his nose!

4. MAKE AN INSPIRING SPEECH

General Magmar is the most eloquent speaker in the monster world. But monsters don't care about his big, fancy words. They just like when he burps. A loud blech is highly motivational for monsters.

5. HIGH-FIVE, MONSTER!

Monsters lose more battles than they win (thanks to those pesky NEXO Knights), so Magmar always boosts morale with positive re-enforcement.

6. NEVER GIVE UP! NEVER SURRENDER!

Actually, the word "never" has a different meaning for monsters: "Never give up . . . until it gets really hard fighting those NEXO Knights, then run away!"

7. WHEN ALL ELSE FAILS . . . MAGMA CHIP COOKIES

The general's famous, boiling-hot, Magma Chip Cookies inspire unconditional loyalty and obedience. They not only melt in your mouth, they melt your entire mouth!

The Marquis de Seaweed

JOB:
Master of the Sea Monsters!

WHAT THE BOOK OF MONSTERS CALLS HIM:
"The Hired Kelp"

FAVORITE SAYING:
"My enemy's anemone is my enemy too!"

WHAT HE KEEPS IN HIS TREASURE CHEST:
Sand dollars

LITTLE KNOWN FACT:
Once dated a sea urchin (it didn't work out)

h no! I must've sprung a leak! No, wait . . . it's one of my Sea Monsters! I forgot to mention this, but Magma beasts are not the only creatures you'll find in my pages. Sea Monsters live here, too, traveling on pirates ships fueled by electric eels.

This is their leader, the Marquis de Seaweed. Kind of a pretentious title if you ask me. But he swings a nasty trident, and his pet piranha, Shredder, just turned three of my chapters into confetti! But don't worry — those were the really good chapters with the magic spells and secrets. You wouldn't want those, would you? Ha! Of course you would! That's what I love about these monsters! They ruin ALL your fun!

This soggy sea monster is really all wet. Ha! I made a joke? All wet? See what I did there?

— M.

Hey, stop stealing those fish, you Lava Monster in diving gear! This page was supposed to be a tour of the Marquis de Seaweed's home! By the way, he has a very stylish, three-bedroom, two-bath shipwreck, with plenty of skylights, an indoor/outdoor octopus, and bay windows that are actually in the bay!

FOR SALE!

It's priced well below
market — about 300, watery,
feet below market in fact. I'd show you
more if this Lava Monster wasn't interrupting
my open house. Did I mention that when I'm not trying to
take over the Kingdom, I, THE BOOK OF MONSTERS, am also
a licensed Real Estate Agent of Monsters? So if you ever need
to sell your haunted castle, sunken ship, or dark and scary cave, just
give me a call. I always get results . . . Well, except for today.

Merlok and His Library

Merlok's library: it was — you guessed it! — filled with books. It was more like a prison for me. I couldn't wait to jail-break that musty ol' place. Finally, Jestro helped me out and freed me from Mer-loser's magical bondage. I do miss the book group on Fridays . . . We used to exchange spells, incantations, and talk about how we'd rather be doing some evil instead of just talkin' about it.

BOOK ELEVATORS
Okay, these things go up and down so you can get books. Pretty cool, really. I always wanted a place on the top shelf with a view.

THE BOOK "PRISON"
This is where I sat trapped in a force field for years and years. I didn't get out for fresh air at all!

A BIG BOOK
Ah, this is the dictionary of
my dreams. Look at her binding –
those endpapers! She's really
something, isn't she?
Merlok always kept us apart.

BOOKSHELVES
Shelves and shelves of
books on all kinds of dopey,
goody-goody magic stuff like,
How to Conjure Unicorns and
How to be as Happy as a Pixie.

SECRET BOOK DOOR
This shelf is really a secret doorway that leads to
a secret passage that leads . . . someplace SECRET!
Stop asking me where!

MERLOK'S DESK
What a mess, huh?
This is the only thing I like
about Merlok – his terribly
messy desk.

MERLOK'S CRYSTAL BALL
He used to use his crystal ball when
he went bowling. Don't tell him I told you.

MORE BOOKS
Look, he's got MORE
BOOKS stashed over here!
What an egghead.

eat a lot of books. I'm hungry. Um, hungry for knowledge. Well, evil knowledge. I wanna know how to make my badness even worse. That's what I get when I stuff evil books down my throat and gobble 'em up. Mmmmm. Evil tastes sooo good. Let me give you some specifics . . .

THE BOOK OF EVIL

Hey, the title says it all. Evil, nasty, and downright bad with an aftertaste of horribleness. Also a touch of caramel for some reason. One of my favorite meals ever.

THE BOOK OF DECEPTION

You think I ate this book? Maybe I was just fooling you? Ha! See what THE BOOK OF DECEPTION lets me do? Deceive you! And let me tell you, this book was deceptively high in calories. Yeesh.

THE BOOK OF CHAOS

Whoa, what a tasty treat! Up is down, warm is cold, black is white . . . anything goes with this chaotic mess of a magic book. It tastes like, well, everything all at once. Total chaos.

THE BOOK OF FEAR
Are you scared yet? Well, I was when Jestro wanted to stuff this book down my gullet. It's pretty scary. What'd it taste like, you ask? It tasted like fear. (By that I mean chicken. Fear pretty much tastes like chicken.)

THE BOOK OF DESTRUCTION
This fiber-filled meal just about wrecked me. But that's its thing — destruction. Hence the title. Duh. Destruction really blows out the taste buds. BOOM!

THE BOOK OF REVENGE
"Revenge is a book that is best served cold." You know, like a cucumber sandwich. This magic book totally made me want to get back at everyone who'd done me wrong. And that's a lot of people (and monsters, and kings, and wizards . . .).

SOME NOTES TO MYSELF ABOUT THIS KOOKY BOOK, BY ME, JESTRO, THE AUTHOR OF THESE NOTES

(not, however, the writer of this book)

THE BOOK OF MONSTERS HAS BAD BREATH. I'LL TRY TO JAM A TUBE OF TOOTHPASTE DOWN HIS THROAT OR TRICK HIM INTO EATING "THE BOOK OF MINTS" OR SOMETHING.

null
San'
dolo
vers
null
mol
reiu
di t
et e

JESTRO

REMEMBER, IF YOU DON'T LIKE WHAT THE BOOK HAS TO SAY, JUST TURN THE PAGE AND MOVE ON.

First off, Jestro, I believe you can be really good at being bad. You might say I believe in you. In me. In us...whatever! Why are you talking to me like I'm soft in the head?! (Only my hat is soft.)

So, do I trust this crazy, ol' Book of Monsters? Well, yes, I guess I do. He is the only one who's actually trying to help me improve myself. He says I can be really, really bad and that makes me feel good.

Trying to get to know all these Lava Monsters and spells and evil things is hard work. Even harder than learning to juggle. Hmm... I wonder if I could juggle monsters? Maybe Globlins, but never Beast Master. He'd get pretty mad.

I should find a cookbook to feed this silly book so that he can make some nice sauces for all these magic books he's forced to swallow all the time. I would get tired of the taste of paper, if it were me. (Similar thought: do fish ever get tired of seafood?)

When I take over the Kingdom of Knighton, I'll make THE BOOK OF MONSTERS the "Lord of Libraries." He'd like that.

I'm so MAD! I just found out THE BOOK OF MONSTERS is reading all my PRIVATE NOTES that I'm scribbling in here! I guess, technically, I'm scribbling them inside HIM, so he can't help himself. Hey... are you reading this note, too, you nosy book?!

THE BOOK OF MONSTERS IS PRETTY MUCH MY FAVORITE TEACHER EVER. SURE, HE'S FIENDISH, BUT IT'S REALLY FOR MY OWN GOOD. IF I JUST PRACTICE AND READ AND LISTEN I CAN BE THE WORST BAD GUY IN THE WORLD!!!

"SHUT YOUR COVER, BOOK" is always a good comeback.

It's not a bookmark, it's his TONGUE.

Mushlord the Marauder

'know, my Lava and Sea Monsters may seem tough, but you haven't truly experienced monstery badness until you've gotten lost in the dark woods with a Forest Monster. These guys are 100 percent, all-natural, free-range EVIL! Meeting one of these organically grown beasts is like getting poison ivy on your soul! It itches and spreads, and you can't do anything about it except cry to your mother!

So start crying, kids, 'cause I'm gonna introduce you to Mushlord the Marauder. He'll either hit you with Fungalibur — his powerful sword made of fungus — or besiege you with a Storm of Spores. What's so bad about that? His spores grow into man-eating mushrooms! Ha!!!

BATTLE CRY:
"There be Fungus Among-us!"
FAVORITE WEAPON:
'shrooms of Doom
HAS NIGHTMARES ABOUT:
Weedkiller and lawn mowers
LOVES LISTENING TO:
Moldy Oldies
LITTLE KNOWN FACT:
His mother was a truffle

Loggerhead

ou know that saying: "Every great oak was once a little nut?" I have a new saying: "THIS TREE IS JUST NUTS!" Completely bonkers. Instead of a brain, Loggerhead has a cranky woodpecker nesting on his head that tells him where to go. Two pecks for "turn right," one peck for "turn left."

Sometimes the bird just gets carried away with its pecking and Loggerhead spins in circles. But look out if Loggerhead ever attacks — he can be an unstoppable battering ram, or a log-rolling "bulldozer." And if he's really mad, he'll give you the WORST splinter ever! Yeeoww!

Ol' Loggerhead is as wooden as a, um, well, block of wood. Please note: he doesn't like Lava Monsters . . . they burn him up.

— M.

LOVES TO: Log in, log out
FAVORITE SNACK: Wood Chips
SUBSCRIBES TO: Driftwood Daily
WEAKNESSES: He is easily "stumped";
Yelling "timber" will make him fall over

MAGIC SPELLS AND INCANTATIONS
(TESTED BY JESTRO)

So, I've found all kinds of crazy spells and incantations in this Book of Monsters. Some work, some don't; some make monsters, others just make trouble. Just be careful, whatever you do, or you might turn yourself into a monster!

Scary, Scary Monsters, come forth and serve me! Make the folks around us wet their pants and flee!

Greedy, greedy Monsters, come out and steal some stuff. Loot and loot and plunder... you can never have enough!

Chaos, Chaos Monster, come out and act real crazy. Make those NEXO Knights look, dumb and slow and lazy.

Angry, angry Monsters, come forth and be real mad! Get so filled with anger you'll be very, very bad!

Destructive, giant Monsters,
come out and bash some stuff!
Pound the castle walls until,
they yell, "we've had enough!"

Monsters, monsters, monsters
here's the great new ploy:
come outta that ol' book
and let's destroy, destroy, DESTROY!

The Bookkeeper

et me tell you, it's pretty amazing being an all-powerful, magical Book of Monsters. Except for one thing: books don't have legs! Not to worry though, I summoned this handy little underling – I mean, uh . . . bookkeeper – out of my magic pages. He just LOVES carrying me everywhere.

He may look completely exhausted and terrified, but that's just the way he smiles, right? Take a look at what he wrote about me in these pages I stole – I mean, borrowed – from his diary. Maybe I should replace him? You carried me pretty nicely before, dear reader. Don't suppose you're free to be my new underling . . . I mean, BOOKKEEPER?

THE BOOKKEEPER DIARY

MONDAY ENTRY

Dear Diary,

Ugh. Guess what I did today? That's right. I carried Master, THE BOOK OF MONSTERS, all over Knighton, again! My legs feel like soggy fish sticks, and my feet have blisters on them the size of a Bloblin! I need to do something else with my life. That's why I'm writing this diary. Thank you for listening, Diary. YOU'RE MY BEST FRIEND....

WEDNESDAY ENTRY
Dear Dailairy,
Today I had a dream that I could fly like a bird. I flew all over the kingdom, so happy and free. And then I woke up. Master was flapping his covers at me, wanting me to carry him across the forest so he could yell at Jestro. Again. I wanted to cry, but my tears just turned to steam. Isn't that the worst?

FRIDAY ENTRY
Dear Diary,
Yep, you guessed it - I carried the Master again. Here, there, everywhere. And the Master ate another evil book too! Doesn't he realize that every book adds 10-15 pounds to his waistline - and another 10-15 pounds to my aching back!?!

SATURDAY ENTRY
Dear Diary,
Today the Master finally said something NICE to me!!! He called me, HIS ARMS AND LEGS. It made me feel like I was "part of the team." Like I had a purpose. I am the Master's arms and legs! I love this job! Guess I don't need you anymore, Diary. I have my new best friend - who I call "Master," because, well, he IS my MASTER. ISN'T THAT THE BEST?

Beast Master

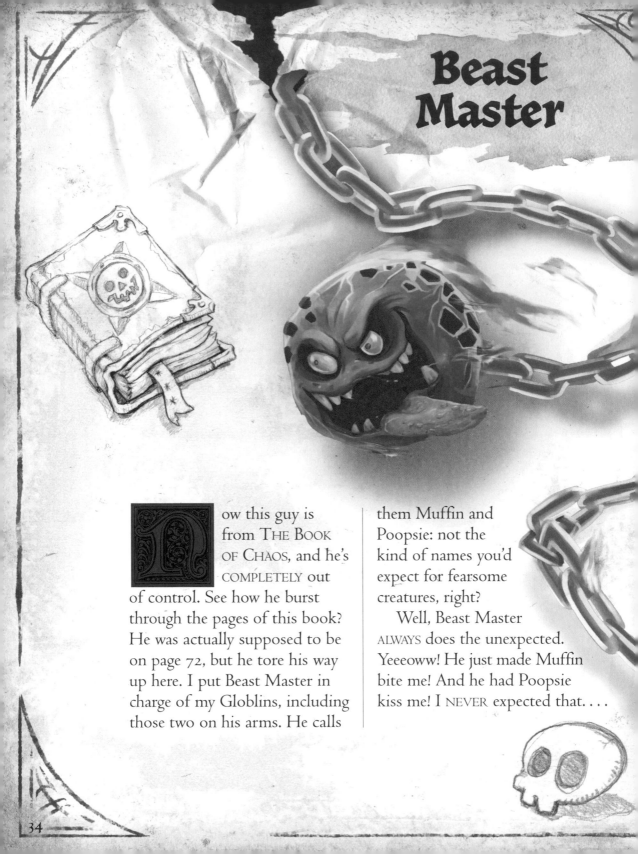

ow this guy is from THE BOOK OF CHAOS, and he's COMPLETELY out of control. See how he burst through the pages of this book? He was actually supposed to be on page 72, but he tore his way up here. I put Beast Master in charge of my Globlins, including those two on his arms. He calls them Muffin and Poopsie: not the kind of names you'd expect for fearsome creatures, right?

Well, Beast Master ALWAYS does the unexpected. Yeeeoww! He just made Muffin bite me! And he had Poopsie kiss me! I NEVER expected that. . . .

JOB: Globlin Wrangler
FAVORITE SAYING: "Grrrrr"
FAVORITE BOOK:
Book of Chaos
LITTLE KNOWN FACT:
He secretly winks at everyone
with his eyepatch-covered eye
THING THAT MAKES
HIM MOST ANGRY:
When monsters give him
mittens for gifts

Globlins, Bloblins

and the Scurriers

36

ook, every truly evil mastermind needs a manic mass of mindless attackers to send out on a whim. Me? I've got not one, but three different, demented hordes to choose from: Globlins, Bloblins, and Scurriers.

Need a mass of bouncing, lava-fueled minions? Call in a swarm of Globlins. What do you do if you're a little Globlin and you want to be bigger? You join together with two-dozen of your closest Globlin friends to form a Bloblin. You need some arms and legs? Call Scurriers! They do all the grunt work: carrying things, throwing things, kicking things.

None of these guys are particularly strong or bright. But when they swarm together . . . well, they're still not particularly bright. But they can totally MESS YOU UP! You hearing this, NEXO KNIGHTS?-ARE YOU?!!?

GLOBLINS' DAY PLANNER

6.00 — Wake up. Complain about Beast Master snoring again.

6.00⁵ — Beast Master overhears complaints. Claims, "I don't snore!" No one believes him.

6.15 — First cup of molten magma. Brush teeth with lava. Pour sulfur into eyes.

6.25 — Lava shower. Burned the shower curtain again!

6.30 — Check in with Beast Master. Tell him his muffins "Taste delicious," even though they are hard as rocks - and not in a good way.

6.35–7.00 — Scare-aerobics. Exercise scare muscles. Do cardio-intensive cycle of tongue snaps and fang barks.

7.00 — Morning briefing: who is getting attacked today? Oh, what a surprise - it's the NEXO Knights and some helpless villagers. Yeahhhh!

Pillage and plunder. | Break for lunch. | Pillage and plunder.

5.30 pm Review and critique the day's pillaging and plundering.

6.00 pm Dinner: barbecue. Again?

6.30 pm Dessert: cream of steam. Again?

TV time. Knighton's Funniest Monsters and Totally Hidden Holograms.

~~**7.00 pm**~~ Hot Tub Party! Woo-hoo!
   8.00 pm

Sleep... if you can. Hope Beast Master doesn't snore all night again!

Book of Monsters' Thoughts After Eating The Book of Chaos

Ow. Just scarfed down THE BOOK OF CHAOS. It's good . . . It's bad. I don't know what to make of it, other than some crazy, chaotic, wacky monsters that will basically be out of control! I wanna be out of control! BLEEEECH! What an aftertaste! Tastes like honey mixed with garlic! Chaos can be hard to swallow.

Now I'm gonna make some totally chaotic Scurriers, just so they can run around and do whatever they want.

This crazy chaos book likes wreaking havoc with the weather: it's raining, it's snowing . . . it's blowing hot air. Today's weather report? Who knows?

So, Jestro the Evil has just ordered the Chaos Monsters to build him an evil vehicle. What is he thinking?! It'll be a chaotic mess!

I finally had to call forth Beast Master to take charge of these chaotic, hot, jumpy monsters. He'd better get 'em in line . . . and fast!

Whiparella

ow THIS monster is SCARY! I want to tell you her name, but every time I try, it comes out like this:

Whiparella

See? I'm shivering in fear!

And watch out for her whip: one touch of its venomous barbs and you'll be facing your deepest, darkest fears. "Oh, Book of Monsters, how is such a thing possible?" you ask. Well, it's like this: the poison in her whip interacts with your brain and finds the one thing that frightens you most. Then her Spider-Globlins confront you with it!

So if she whips you and learns you're afraid of the dark, her Spider-Globlins will block out all the light around you.

If – WHIPCRACK – you hate rabbits, her Spider-Globlins will form into a ferocious carnivorous bunny! If you fear failure, like a certain annoying NEXO Knight I know – WHIPCRACK – the Spider-Globlins will make you fail again and again and again.

JOB: Bringing on the Terror with a capital T

FAVORITE BOOK: Book of Fear

WEAPON OF CHOICE: Her whip and her transforming Spider-Globlins

WHAT REALLY BUGS HER: When a certain annoying knight calls her, "Wimperella"

What's in Whiparella's Closet

- Hooks to hold Whip of Fear
- Scrunchies of Fear (keeps her hair in frighteningly good shape)
- Lava Lands: Spring Break '92 T-shirt
- A book: How to Care for Spider-Globlins
- Frilly pink dress with flowers (shhh!)

The Sing-along Siren of Seaguard

Quick! Quick! Plug your ears! If you listen to the siren's song too long, you'll be taken in by her magical singing. I'm sorry . . . what did you say? I've got my ears plugged.

— M.

his siren is always like, "oh, look at my fancy tail!" Yeah, we get it . . . she can swim like a fish. And usually she swims right over to the nearest karaoke joint. All Sirens love to sing. They usually use their eerie songs to hypnotize sailors.

The Siren of Seaguard, however, makes everyone sing along with her party favorites: For He's a Jolly Good Monster; 99 Bottles of Fear on the Wall; and Row, Row, Row Your Hoverboat. And then while you're distracted . . . she attacks! Or she just lets the song get stuck in your head. Either way — you're doomed.

The Siren's Lyrics to "Row, Row, Row Your Hoverboat"

Row, row, row your Hoverboat,
Gently through the air.
You know that rowing's useless,
When you're floating everywhere.

Row, row, row your Hoverboat,
Gently 'cross the land.
Still rowing? What part of HOVERboat,
Don't you understand?

NICKNAME:
Surf and Turf Songstress
FAVORITE SAYING:
"All together now!"
GOT HER START IN:
The Coral Chorale
WON FIRST PLACE ON:
Lava Lands Idol
LITTLE KNOWN FACT:
Puts her pants on one fin at a time

ear reader, you're halfway through this book. Don't you feel like you need a holiday right about now? I know a lovely tropical island in the middle of nowhere.

Only . . . it's NOT an island, it's a terrifying Sea Monster with palm trees stuck on its head. Once you're relaxing on the sand, this island will rise up and bare its snarling fangs! Surprise! That's no beach – it's the forehead of The Behemoth of Brine, the largest of ALL my monsters. Hey, guess who just won an all-expense-paid trip here? That's right: the NEXO Knights, courtesy of a travel agent called . . . THE BOOK OF MONSTERS. Ha!

The Behemoth of Brine

LOVES: Ruining your holiday!
HATES: When life vests get stuck in his teeth
ONCE DATED: An iceberg
FAVORITE SAYING: "Snackin' like a Kraken!"
WHAT HE WRITES ON POSTCARDS: "Wish you were here – SO I COULD EAT YOU!"

The Book of Love

Here's a letter I wrote to the dictionary in Merlok's library. I really thought she was the prettiest book I'd ever seen! Uh, after I wrote the letter, I swallowed a thesaurus just so I could impress her with my new language skills. Ain't I smart?

Miriamiriamiria Miriamiriamiriamiriamiriamiria miriamiria

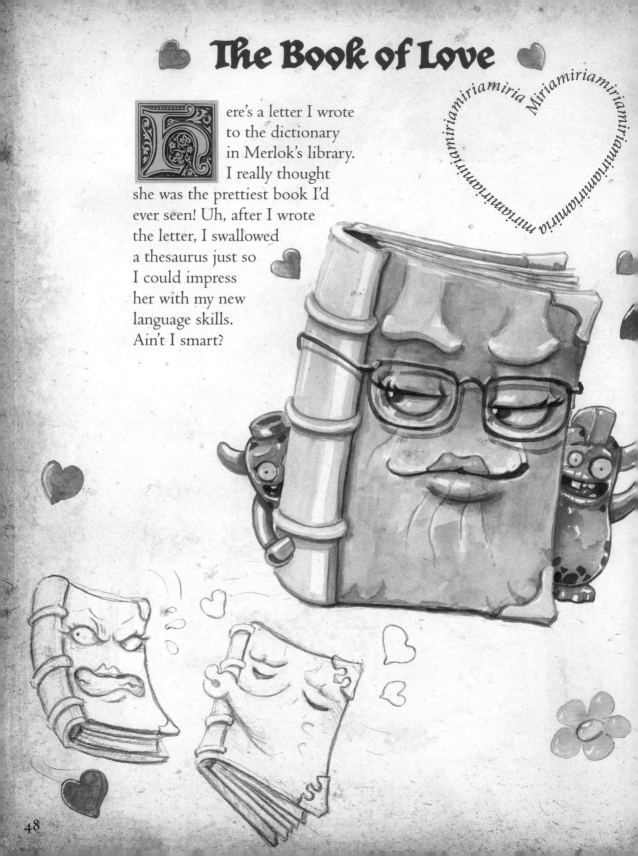

DEAR MIRIAM,

Have you ~~seen~~ "*gazed upon*" the ~~moon~~ "*yon sailing orb*" ~~tonight~~ "*this whimsical dusk-time?*" It's as ~~beautiful~~ "*resplendent*" as your ~~leather-bound cover~~ "*goatskin-tooled parchment protectors.*" I'd ~~really like~~ "*particularly cotton*" to ~~take a walk in your fountain of word knowledge~~ "*stroll amongst your repository of word inventories.*" I mean, ~~you're so smart~~ "*thou art briskly shrewd*" and have such ~~excellent diction~~ "*meritorious verbiage.*" I ~~really like~~ "*undoubtedly delight in*" your "K" to "M" sections. I've ~~admired~~ "*cherished*" you from ~~far away~~ "*afar*" all ~~these years~~ "*through this epoch*" and I know that I finally have to ~~say something~~ "*give verbiage to my contemplation . . .*"

But what can I say to the ~~girl~~ "*maiden of lists*" that doesn't sound like ~~small talk~~ "*tiny speak?*" Who has such an ~~attractive~~ "*enchanting*" gold-leaf binding? I ~~hope~~ "*daydream*" you don't think I'm ~~monstrous~~ "*fiendish*" for saying so, but let's ~~get together~~ "*converge*" after torches-out and I could ~~read~~ "*peruse*" you some spells. Or ~~talk~~ "*orate*" about the, uh, ~~weather~~ "*meteorological events.*" Maybe you could ~~improve~~ "*augment*" my linguistic ~~skills~~ "*competence.*" I'd ~~like~~ "*venerate*" that.

Yours Very ~~Truly~~ "*verbosely,*"
THE BOOK OF MONSTERS
(two shelves over on the left in the special
holo-containment field to prevent me
from unleashed "*fomenting*" evil.)

Leave me alone, you dusty weirdo!
— Miriam

49

Deadwood & Knot

 ee that big brute there? His name's Deadwood, because all his leaves died ages ago . . . along with most of his brain cells. It happened after he removed one of his main branches to make that club. Can you say, "Duhhhh?" Luckily, he has that knot of wood in his belt area to do the thinking for him. The little guy's name is actually Addison Posh St. Claire III, but Deadwood just calls him "Knot."

Because . . . well, he's a knot of wood, and he's NOT Deadwood. I wouldn't exactly call them a dynamic duo, but if you need to put the "Fear of the Forest" in your foes, these two will beat anyone in their path to a pulp – a WOOD pulp that is. No lumbering around for them. Ha!

DEADWOOD

<u>HOBBIES:</u>
Wood carving
<u>DAILY HABIT:</u>
Campfires!
<u>FAVORITE SAYING:</u>
"Creeeeak!"
<u>DISLIKES:</u>
All this fairy dust

KNOT

<u>HOBBIES:</u>
Yelling, "Stop carving me, Deadwood!"
<u>DAILY HABIT:</u> Putting out Deadwood's burning limbs
<u>FAVORITE SAYING:</u>
"'Creeeeak' is not even a word!"
<u>DISLIKES:</u>
"It's not fairy dust, it's your SAWDUST!"

Baron Badwood

Talk about low-hanging fruit, this Forest Monster grows his own poison apples! One bite, and it's nighty-night, NEXO Knight. Sweet dreams – NOT! (Hey, if you're dumb enough to eat produce growing out of a monster's head, you deserve a few nightmares.)

Baron Badwood actually got his name from his ferocious smell. He stinks! Like rotten eggs mixed with old sewage . . . and sweaty NEXO KNIGHT TUBE SOCKS. Flies follow him everywhere!

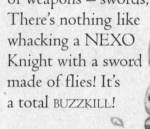

But the Baron's worked out how to control these bugs with his "stink sap." He makes the flies swarm into the shape of weapons — swords, spears, whips. There's nothing like whacking a NEXO Knight with a sword made of flies! It's a total BUZZKILL!

LOVES TO: Branch out
HATES: Laying down roots
HAIRCUTS REQUIRE:
A chainsaw
FAVORITE SAYING:
"The apple doesn't fall far from the head."
SECRET FACT:
His bark is worse than his bite

Ah, Baron Badwood. All bark, no bite. I wish he would make like a tree . . . and leave.
— M.

53

Lavaria

Not, hot, hot Magma Monsters, it's Lavaria! She is one monster spy "that can set your heart on fire." (Did I mention that she's hot?) She knows how to work a situation: getting information, sneaking around, pretending to be someone she's not (which is really helpful around those kooky, uptight knights.)

I usually want Lavaria brought forth from my pages when we really need to get one over on those goody-goodies, or when we need to try to trick Merlok 2.0. (Trust me, that guy ain't easy to fool. But Lavaria's sooo good, she's actually managed it a couple of times.)

Oh, my, yes . . . Lavaria. She is, um, how do I put this? She's pretty hot. You can't believe a word she says because she's an excellent spy. Remember that.
— M.

JOB TITLE:
Monster Super Spy
BEST SKILL:
Master of disguise
FAVORITE SAYING:
"Why don't you tell me about that?"
IN HER PAST:
She studied drama at monster school
LITTLE KNOWN FACT:
She's got a crush on Jestro

NEXO Knights

s you know, I'm training this fool Jestro on how to be bad – REALLY bad. It's not easy. He used to be such a goody-two-slippers!

When Jestro was part of the royal court, King Halbert asked him to describe how he felt about all these so-called NEXO Knights. Look at the drivel he wrote! Then I asked him to do the same thing after a few intense cram sessions at my SCHOOL OF EVIL! Muhahahaha! Observe the student's performance.

Clay Moorington

Hey Monsters,

What a buffoon this guy is! He even laughs at my jokes when they're not funny! Clay has the personality of dirt. Or should I say clay. Ha, ha! And he won't stop blah-blahing about his precious Knight's Code.

The only thing he inspires me to do is cover my ears with hot lava rocks. Yeah, that hurts, but not as much as listening to this NEXO-Know-it-all.

Macy Halbert

DEAR KING HALBERT,
What can I say? Your daughter Macy is a-Mace-ing! What a princess! And what a knight! She can do it all! Macy is like the big sister I always wanted — but with awesome weapon skills! You should be sooo proud of her.

Hey Monsters,
What can I say? That Macy is MESSED UP! Is she a princess? Is she a knight? I just call her Lady Epic Fail. She's like the big sister I NEVER wanted. And if we were related, I'd tell her, "Stop stinkin' up the kingdom, Sis!" That dumb King Half-a-Brain should be so ashamed of her!

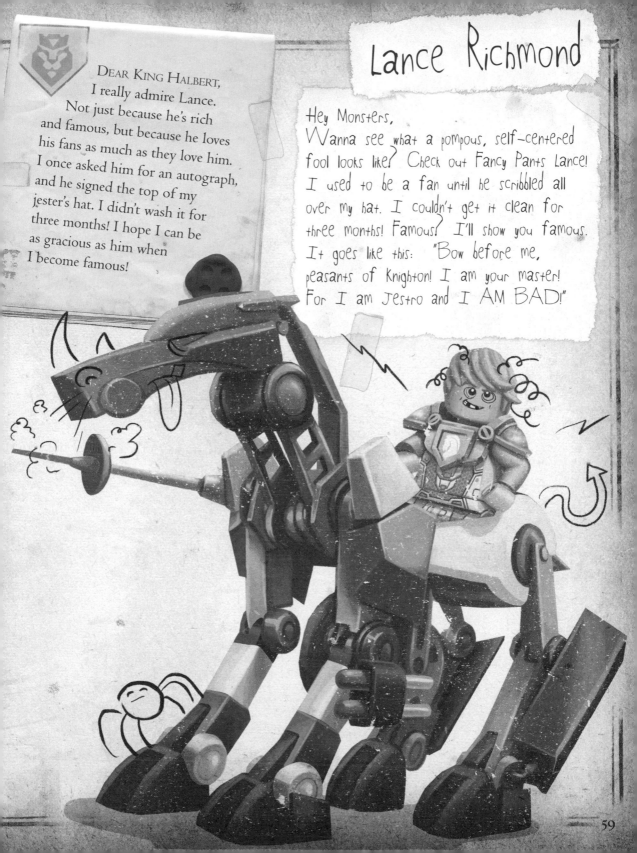

Lance Richmond

DEAR KING HALBERT,
I really admire Lance. Not just because he's rich and famous, but because he loves his fans as much as they love him. I once asked him for an autograph, and he signed the top of my jester's hat. I didn't wash it for three months! I hope I can be as gracious as him when I become famous!

Hey Monsters,
Wanna see what a pompous, self-centered fool looks like? Check out Fancy Pants Lance! I used to be a fan until he scribbled all over my hat. I couldn't get it clean for three months! Famous? I'll show you famous. It goes like this: "Bow before me, peasants of Knighton! I am your master! For I am Jestro and I AM BAD!"

Aaron Fox

DEAR KING HALBERT,
I only wish I could be as brave as Aaron Fox. He is completely fearless, embracing danger the way some of us embrace our cuddly toy dragons at night when we're scared of the dark. I'm not saying I do that. At least, not if the knight light is working. As for Aaron? Dark, light — it doesn't matter. He is the extreme of extremes . . . Unstoppable. Unbreakable. And unforgettable.

Hey Monsters,
Forget this Aaron guy. We zcan totally break him and stop him. I'm tired of him whipping around the kingdom on his hover shield like a squirebot with its head unscrewed. He wants danger? I'll show him danger! I'll show him EXTREME JESTRO! Take that, dude. And when I say, dude, I actually mean, NEXO-Fool who I will soon destroy!

DEAR KING HALBERT,
Axl is not just big – he's bighearted. One time, I was eating all by myself in the castle commissary. I felt so alone, until Axl joined me – and he wouldn't leave until we'd finished every plate! I'd love to hug him, but if he hugged me back, he'd probably break my spine. And I need my spine. It holds up my head, and makes my shirts fit properly.

AXL

Hey Monsters,
Spines are overrated. Am I right, Globlins? Now let's talk about Axl. The only reason he joined me for dinner that time was so he could EAT ALL MY FOOD! What a pig! I used to think he had a big heart. Now I realize it was just his big stomach! I may pillage and plunder, but that NEXO-Numbnut stole my cake!

The Fortrex

So, the knights have this big, dopey rolling fortress called THE FORTREX. It's a total pain in my back cover because Merlok 2.0 lives there and he can send out his NEXO Power whenever the knights need it to beat me and my monsters.

Do I sound jealous? I AM! Who wouldn't want a fortress that you can drive around the kingdom!

On top of this thing they've got? A big crossbow they call "The Bowtrex." Yeah, they think puttin' an X into everything makes it high-tech.

I've tried throwing flaming monsters against the walls but they just slide right off.

This thing used to be the King's royal RV, then they converted it into this thing. It's got a kitchen, a workout room, an armory and even a lounge — mainly for that lazy Richmond guy.

FORTREX FEATURES

- Command Center – Where the NEXO Magic happens!
- Holo Training Room – Where they pretend to fight stuff
- Kitchen – Home to a squirebot named Chef Éclair
- Garage – Their vehicle stash
- Lounge – Comfy chairs, TV, video games
- Giant Treads – Ready to roll on any terrain

I ain't into the super high-tech of this thing. I prefer good, ol' fashioned monster magic. I guess that should be bad, ol' fashioned monster magic?

OK, they've got these fancy-schmancy NEXO Shields that download NEXO Powers from Merlok 2.0 Whatever . . .

Aaron actually uses his NEXO Shield as a hover shield and he plays jammin' tunes in his helmet. He's so cool it makes me hot, hot, HOT!

See these weapons? When they get powered up by that NEXO Power, they make my monsters go ethereal and then they're sent back into me . . . and it gives me indigestion.

This NEXO Armor they wear also powers up. Just stop it already! I'm gonna prove, one way or another, that nasty magic Lava Monsters can beat all this teched-up nonsense. Feel me?

This front part is a drawbridge that leads inside. They've even got room to park their high-tech vehicles in there. And they don't have to pay for parking, either!

Ava Prentis

This little student knight has a mind for computers, coding, and keeping Merlok 2.0 up and running. Can't she just let it go, then Merlok 2.0 will crash and fade away? Probably not, with her mind for machine languages on that rolling fortress. I mean, she's only a little kid, but she's smarter than any monsters I've got. And, usually, smart beats stupid. I'm just sayin'.

I don't know what she's doing here and I don't wanna know. Suffice to say it's probably something that saves Merlok 2.0's bacon.

Typing, typing, typing! It makes my hands cramp up just thinking about it. And I don't even have hands!

She keeps that musty, old magician in tip-top virtual shape. If Ava weren't around he'd be totally unorganized and fragmented.

KNIGHTS' ACADEMY STUDENTS

- They learn to be knights
- They're more high-tech than ever
- They've got? all kinda "skillz" as they say
- Gonna take NEXO Power to the next level
- Have to study AND help the NEXO Knights

She gets the knights ready to get their NEXO Powers. I wish I could sneak a SCURRIER in to pretend to be her. Wait a minute . . . that's an excellent plan!

Robin Underwood

his kid totally bugs me. He's enthusiastic, he's cheerful, and he can tinker together almost anything. And then the knights use it to kick some monster butt! He's only a freshman at the Knights' Academy and I wish he'd take his studyin' more seriously … because that would mean he's not helping the knights build stuff. He's full of ideas … and I hate all of them.

That NEXO Ultra Armor was all this kid's idea. He even built the stuff. That's "ultra-crazy" in my book!

He built the Bowtrex on top of the rolling fortress. Thanks a lot for that.

Why's he such a wiz with building stuff? Didn't his parents teach him math? How irresponsible.

I'll admit, the kid's pretty handy. I hope he decides to become a plumber and not a knight.

MERLOK 2.0 & NEXO POWERS

Each NEXO Knight has a special weapon. I don't think they're very good at sharing.

Merlok was always nice to me, even though I was a total failure as a magic user. He got me my job as a jester, which didn't work out, because everybody laughed at me all the time. Guess I shoulda realized that was part of the job. Instead, I decided to just let it FREAK ME OUT!

So, when Merlok had to use a mondo magic spell to blow the Book of Monsters and me across the kingdom, he turned himself into Merlok 2.0, some sort of computer digi-magic image.

We thought maybe he was gone, but nooooo, he's become the operating system of the Fortrex.

What a weird world I live in, huh?

Merlok 2.0 sends his digi-magic powers to the NEXO Knights and they can power themselves up with NEXO Power — their weapons, their armor, everything.

It's totally not fair!

This NEXO Power can be downloaded through their shields. It gives them, usually, just the right kind of power to overcome my monsters. But I'm not gonna let their high-tech stuff beat my Magma Monsters. I'm gonna be good at being bad!

That Ava kid keeps the NEXO systems up and running. I'd like to trap her in a magic book just to get her out of the way.

You know, I thought Magma Monsters would be unstoppable, but this NEXO Magic can send them back into the Book of Monsters. It gives him terrible indigestion. Makes me sick, too.

It seems this NEXO Power stuff came about just like, um, magic. But maybe Merlok meant for it to happen. How do I know? All I know is that it's a major pain in my book....the Book of Monsters.

They download new powers all the time depending on what monsters they're facing. I hate how flexible they are. And they don't seem to do any stretching.

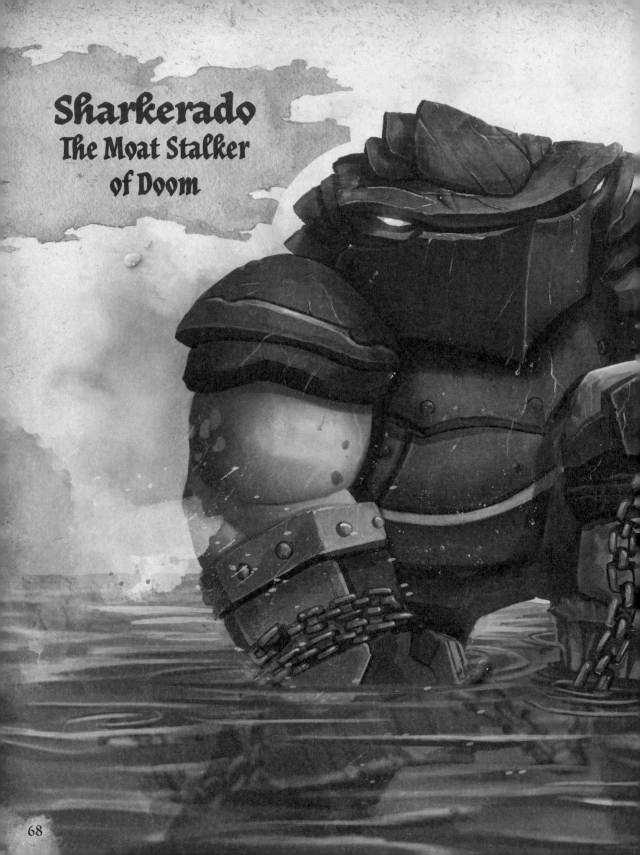

Sharkerado
The Moat Stalker of Doom

et me tell you something about moats — those pretty little pools of water that you find "protecting" our kingdom's fanciest castles. They don't work! Why? One word: SHARKERADO.

This Sea Monster may hail from the ocean's shadowy depths, but he does some of his best work in Knighton's freshwater moats. Think that drawbridge will protect you? Sharkerado will bust through it with his hammerin' hammerhead! Or he'll drag you down with his Morning Star of Shadow. And that's exactly what you'll see: stars. Well, and then you'll say: "Glug-glug-glug." You know, because you'll be underwater . . . face-to-face with . . . SHARKERADO!
THE MOAT STALKER OF DOOM!

LIVES IN: A sunken pirate ship
LOVES: The ocean's shadowy depths
HATES: No phone reception in shadowy depths; keeps missing text messages
FAVORITE SNACK: Crackers and chum
FAVORITE ATTACK MOVE:
Falling Star

69

Chef Savage

am The Book of Monsters and I love to eat evil books. That's just what I do. The Book of Evil, The Book of Chaos, The Book of Fear — I have devoured these and many more scrumptiously evil volumes.

But one menacing masterpiece has eluded me all these years: The Cookbook of Evil. It was written by a Sea Monster pirate named Chef Savage. (Pronounce it like you speak French: "Sa-vahhh-jjj!") His waiters are named Poop and Deck. (Pronounce them like you DON'T speak French: "Poop" and "Deck.") For those of us in the Dark Realm, Chef Savage is a virtuoso of the culinary arts. He even cooks better than General Magmar! Of course, I don't care about his Lava Soufflés or Hemlock Smoothies. I just want to eat his cookbook — oh, those sweet, succulent pages of evil. I would say more, but I'm soooo hungry my drool is making all my words fade

Chez Chef Savage

— MENU —

Truffled serpent bladder, grilled to perfection	Your mortal soul, plus tip
Cyclops cornea, dipped in chocolate	Your mortal soul, plus tip
Artisanal bat whiskers a la scampi	Your mortal soul, plus tip
Finger-licking troll fingers, w/ blue cheese	4.95
Southwestern-style gargoyle wings	Your mortal soul, plus tip
Mouth-watering unicorn burger	Your mortal soul, plus tip
Hand-crafted elf hands (al dente)	Your mortal soul, plus tip
Zesty witch's wart, infused with sea salts	Happy Hour Special: 6.95
World famous ogre knuckles	Your mortal soul, plus tip
Oven-roasted poison (voted best in the Lava Lands)	Free with every meal

Welcome to Chez Chef Savage.
Enjoy our food. And let your servers,
Poop and Deck know if you have any allergies -
because they LOVE to make you sick!
Please also check
with your servers for
the
Specials of the Day.

Poop & Deck

Monster Vehicles

Hey, those shiny-brained heroes aren't the only ones with stuff to drive around the kingdom. We've got some fiery, monster vehicles that can burn up the roads! It's actually the most fun part of my job to drive into a pleasant, happy, little hamlet and then BURN IT TO THE GROUND! (After pillaging it of its riches, first.)

This is the Evil Mobile. I thought up the name, but Jestro wants the credit. It was built by Chaos Monsters so it's a bit of a mess, but it's still one hot, dangerous ride!

Globlins can jump into the big back tires and give us a fiery boost when we need it.

There's even a prison cell in this thing for, uh, imprisoning things.

It's pulled by Burnzie and Sparkks, and if they don't have enough carbs in the morning, it burns out.

Twin catapults for tossing Globlins and Bloblins. It's really fun to watch them fly and turn up the heat on those goody-goodies!

This is where Jestro drives the thing. He's not a good driver. (Yeah, I said it . . .)

MONSTER VEHICLE ATTRIBUTES

- Mostly made of magma
- Hot, hot, hot!
- Good at mashing villages
- Lots of catapults = lots of Globlin flingin'
- They're gonna set the realm on fire!

General Magmar drives his Siege Machine of Doom. A vehicle and a siege tower in one? That's why he's a general.

Two giant Bloblins are on the front of this Beast Master's Chaos Chariot, waitin' to chomp into anything in their way.

I love these lava nasties! They've got a big Chaos Catapult for flingin' Globlins.

Dame Flora

ou may not realize this, but I, THE BOOK OF MONSTERS, just LOVE receiving flowers — especially if they come from Dame Flora. She's the chief gardener of the Forest Monsters, and her petals always have teeth! Wow! Those floral fangs are sharp! Sniff one of these blossoms and you'll get your face bitten right off!

Then, when someone asks you, "Hey, buddy, where'd your face go?" you'll sound really stupid explaining that it was munched away by some pretty little flower. That's how evil Dame Flora is: she not only hurts you, she embarrasses you too! She always puts the "ow!" in flower.

This is one flower you don't want to pick. Talk about thorny . . . . the last time I encountered Dame Flora she turned all the houseplants against me. — M.

OFFICIAL JOB TITLE:
Horticulturist of Horrors
FAVORITE SLOGAN:
"Slay it with flowers"
SPECIALTY:
Face-eating floral arrangements
BOUQUET CARDS READ:
"Thinking of you . . . without a face!"
LITTLE KNOWN FACT:
Never stops to smell the roses
WEAPON TRIVIA:
Fighting sword doubles as a pruning shear

The Elm of the Dark Realm

Don't ever make
a magic staff from
the branches of the Elm
of the Dark Realm.
That staff will take
over your soul
and make you evil.
Or, sometimes, he'll use
his magic to turn you
into a coffee table.
                — M.

ook around. How many things do you see that are made of wood? Your chair? Your table? Your house? It may just be lumber to you humans, but the Elm of the Dark Realm sees it as his fallen brethren. And he is out for revenge, ruthlessly devouring the bodies and souls of anyone who has ever misused a piece of timber, or even gotten a splinter!

So if you value your survival, stay away from anything made of wood — that includes toothpicks and paper products. Wait a sec . . . I'm a book . . . made of paper. Oh no! RUN AWAYYYYYY!

Bramblina

eh! Ahh! Ouch! I hurt myself just thinking about this prickly Forest Monster and her razor-sharp thorns. She once gave me a hug, and put holes in both my covers! You ever get a ticket punched on a train or a bus? I looked just like that — but with 20 times more holes!

When she's not being a total thorn in my side, Bramblina loves to attack sweet, innocent villagers with her sour Berry Globlins. These guys not only spit exploding seeds, they stain your clothes with berry juice too! And that stuff NEVER comes out! So BEWARE!

NICKNAME:
Barb
BATTLE CRY:
"Shrub-a-Dub-Dub!"
SECRET SKILL:
Her thistles can whistle
GETS ALL HER
RUMORS FROM:
The grapevine
GREATEST FEAR:
Her berries will be turned
into a smoothie!

JESTRO'S TIPS:
HOW TO SUMMON MONSTERS

So, the basic way you summon a scary monster is to wave a magic staff over The Book of Monsters, say some stuff, or sometimes not. It's hard to know what works. I have this really cool staff I found in Merlok's library and it's become my favorite. I've gotten beyond the basic waving of the thing and gotten into more, um, artistic stuff.

1. Know what monster is best for the job. Like, if you want lots of gold, you need greed monsters. If you want lots of wrecking stuff, you need destructive monsters.

2. If I wave the staff over my head, I get over-the-top monsters. It's all in the body language. But don't get too crazy until you get the hang of it.

3. Sometimes, I don't know what I want, so I just call forth a bunch of Globlins and Bloblins and they just bounce around being crazy. That's a good way to start the day.

BIG TIP: Don't start pillaging too early in the morning. One time, I destroyed the Hamlet of Omelette before I got a nice veggie omelette for breakfast, and I was hungry all day.

4. Know who you're summoning. I called out Magmar before I even knew he was a control freak. That guy is constantly trying to overrule me. Who does he think he is? I mean other than a Monster General.

5. Look, Burnzie and Sparkks always seem to disappoint, but they try hard. And, I know they're loyal. So, it's easiest to give them another chance and hope things turn out differently.

Look, be smart: if you need to carry stuff off, make sure you summon Scurriers. Globlins can't carry anything. They have arms.

Flama & Moltor

These two burned their initials in the walls around the King's Castle on a dare. That's monstrous!

— M.

h, I love these guys! Very monstery, very aggressive, very immature. They're twins that are just trying to make a reputation as hot, hot guys. Sure, they can be obnoxious, but together they can also be good at wrecking stuff. And they follow orders well. That's always a positive in an underling — taking direction.

FLAMA
He's covered with flames all the time. He makes a great reading lamp.

You know what they studied? How to set stuff on fire. They got As for that class.

MOLTOR
Big hands. Grip strength
of a Magma Monkey . . . comes
in handy.

They do everything together.
It's a twin-thing.

They were on the pillaging team.
Undefeated. They're winners.

The Lava Monsters
once tried to make peace
with him by accidentally
serving him calamari
at a dinner party.
Turned out to be
his second cousin.
— M.

Mate Squiddybeard

e monsters can be a frightening and unpredictable bunch. But Mate Squiddybeard is a whole new class of dangerous and weird. He used to be a brilliant pirate commander until he got that head injury. Did you ever see someone put a pencil behind their ear so they won't lose it? Well, Squiddybeard did that with his ship's anchor — all 75 tons of it. *Crunch!* He's never been the same since.

Now he's always trying to change the batteries in electric eels, or put horseshoes on seahorses. But if you ever need to take down some annoying NEXO Knight, Squiddybeard will totally deliver a salty assault!

JOB: Confused Commander
NICKNAME: Barnacle Brain
FREQUENTLY ARGUES WITH: Sea buoys
THINKS: Sandbars serve sand drinks
FAVORITE HOBBY: Thumb wrestling jellyfish
ONCE DATED: A piece of coral
FAVORITE SAYING: "Huh?"
LITTLE KNOWN FACT: Loves sushi! But only the kind that grows on fruit trees

When they can't fight NEXO Knights, my monsters
love fighting each other. Check out what happens when
my hot-and-fiery Lava Monsters meet my wet-and-slippery
Sea Monsters! And then when my woody Forest Monsters
come along, they're COMPLETELY stumped!

Fear Globlins!
They've got spider's legs and can
run around and scare off even
the biggest good guy.